Autumn's Emergency

Doggie Tails Series

Autumn's Emergency

Doggie Tails Series

by David M. Sargent, Jr.

Illustrated by Jeane Lirley Huff

Ozark Publishing, Inc.
P.O. Box 228
Prairie Grove, AR 72753

Cataloging-in-Publication Data

Sargent, David M., 1966–
    Autumn's emergency / by David M. Sargent, Jr. ;
illustrated by Jeane Lirley Huff.—Prairie Grove, AR :
Ozark Publishing, c2004.
    p. cm. (Doggie tails series)

    SUMMARY: Autumn comes to the farm and guards
it faithfully.
    ISBN 1-56763-845-7 (hc)
          1-56763-846-5 (pbk)

    [1. Dogs—Fiction. 2. Stories in rhyme.] I. Huff,
Jeane Lirley, 1946–, ill. II. Title.

    PZ8.3.S2355Au 2004
    [E]—dc21   00-012095

Printed in the United States of America

iv

Inspired by

Autumn and all the trouble she finds,
whether looking for it or not.

Dedicated to

Autumn.
You're just a big ole goofball.

Vera, Mary, and Buffy made
A new friend around town.
Her name is Autumn, and she's big and brown.

She came to live with us on the farm.
She's really sweet and does no harm.

I gave her a job, and she does it well.
She guards the farm over hill and dell.

She chases the rabbits, squirrels, and coons,
Then plays with them all day like a big ole goon.

She never eats them or hurts them in any way.
She just wants to make them play the day away.

At night, she gets to sleep in the house.
Although she's big, she's as quiet as a mouse.

One morning early I let her out.
The farm, you see, needed its scout.

On this day, when she came home,
She was tattered and torn and cut to the bone.

Her body looked bad but I could see in her eyes,
It was not yet time to say our good-byes.

We raced to the doctor's to get some help.
She never cried once—nope, not a yelp.

The doctor sewed stitches while I sat and prayed
And remembered all the times
Autie and I had played.

About three weeks later she was as good as new.
And eager to go home because she had a job to do.

She still guards the farm both night and day.
But now she never wanders very far away.

DISCARDED